D0601271
WITHDRAWN

BOING
BOING
BOING
BOING
BOING
BOING

BOING

NICK BRUEL

A NEAL PORTER BOOK
ROARING BROOK PRESS
NEW MILFORD, CONNECTICUT

BOING

TO MORGAN, SAM, & ABBIE

A Neal Porter Book

Published by Roaring Brook Press

Roaring Brook Press is a division of Holtzbrinck Publishing Holdings Limited Partnership

143 West Street, New Milford, Connecticut, 06776

Distributed in Canada by H. B. Fenn and Company Ltd.

Library of Congress Cataloging-in-Publication Data

Bruel, Nick.

Boing! / Nick Bruel. — 1st ed.

p. cm.

Summary: A mother kangaroo and various woodland animals coach her Joey

as she attempts her first jump.

ISBN 1-59643-002-8

[1. Kangaroos—Fiction. 2. Jumping—Fiction.] I. Title.

PZ7.B82832Bo 2004

[E]—dc22 2003018135

Roaring Brook Press books are available for special promotions and premiums.

For details contact: Director of Special Markets, Holtzbrinck Publishers.

First edition November 2004

Printed in China

10 9 8 7 6 5 4 3 2

MUNCH
MUNCH
WATCH
ME!

BOING
BOING
BOING
WOWIE!
YOWIE!
ZOWIE!
CLAP
CLAP
CLAP

NG
BOING

MUNCH
MUNCH
YOUR
TURN!
YOU CAN
DO IT!
IT'S FUN!

COME TO MAMA!

BLOMP
OH DEAR!

BOING
SCRATCH
SCRATCH
BOING
BOING

LIKE THIS!
BOING

IT'S EASY!
BOING
BOING
BOING

BOING

BLOOMP

OH MY!

BOING
DON'T GIVE UP!
BOING
BOING

BOING

BLOP

OH GOLLY!

WHAT DO YOU HAVE IN YOUR POCKET?

I HAVE 1 SOCK,
A CANDYBAR, 2 JACKS,
A TOY DINOSAUR, 3 MARBLES,
A COOL ROCK I FOUND, 4 BUTTONS,
ANOTHER TOY DINOSAUR, 5 CRAYONS,
A BOOK ABOUT ROBOTS, 6 ACORNS,
A DRAWING OF A FLOWER,
MY PIGGY BANK,

A **RED** RIBBON, A YO-YO,

A **YELLOW** RIBBON, MY DOLLY,

A **BLUE** RIBBON, A SPOON, A FEATHER,

A **PURPLE** RIBBON, A PAPER CLIP,

AN **ORANGE** RIBBON,

A **GREEN** RIBBON,

MY HAIRBRUSH,

AND A BANANA.

TRY AGAIN!
BIG BOOK OF ROBOTS

WOWIE!
YOWIE!
ZOWIE!